Jolene's
Back

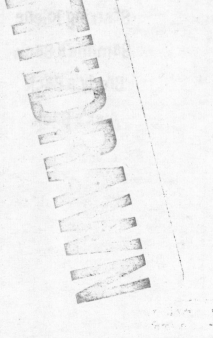

Jolene's Back

—the girl who knows what she wants (and won't stop till she gets it)

Helena Pielichaty

Illustrated by Melanie Williamson

OXFORD
UNIVERSITY PRESS

OXFORD

UNIVERSITY PRESS

Great Clarendon Street, Oxford OX2 6DP

Oxford University Press is a department of the University of Oxford.
It furthers the University's objective of excellence in research, scholarship,
and education by publishing worldwide in

Oxford New York

Auckland Cape Town Dar es Salaam Hong Kong Karachi
Kuala Lumpur Madrid Melbourne Mexico City Nairobi
New Delhi Shanghai Taipei Toronto

With offices in

Argentina Austria Brazil Chile Czech Republic France Greece
Guatemala Hungary Italy Japan Poland Portugal Singapore
South Korea Switzerland Thailand Turkey Ukraine Vietnam

Oxford is a registered trade mark of Oxford University Press
in the UK and in certain other countries

Database right Oxford University Press (maker)

First published 2006

British Library Cataloguing in Publication Data

Data available

ISBN-13: 978-0-19-275380-9
ISBN-10: 0-19-275380-0

3 5 7 9 10 8 6 4 2

Typeset by Palimpsest Book Production Limited,
Polmont, Stirlingshire

Printed in Great Britain by Cox and Wyman Ltd., Reading, Berkshire

Dedicated to:

Bretton Hall College, Wakefield
1948–2007

. . . especially those trained as teachers
during the vintage years
1974–1978

Chapter One

Before I start, if you're a girl reading this, I just want to say something. Last time you heard from me I said I didn't want you to read my stuff if you liked kittens and thought boys were 'cool' and you wore pina colada lip gloss. Well, forget all that. I'm not bothered what you like or what you wear. It's each to their own, isn't it? I'm not going to judge you, just like I wouldn't expect you to judge me because I'm never seen out of my Sunderland AFC shirt and would rather lick a Toon fan's boots than wear lip gloss. No hard feelings then? Mint. Now I've got that off my chest I can start.

Life's a bit mad up here at the moment. Usually when the football season is over I'm a bit lost and bored like, but not this summer term. There's too much going on. I leave primary school this time so there's been loads of stuff to sort out for my new secondary school like uniforms to buy and forms to fill in and bus passes to organize. On top of that there's masses to finish off in class, like taking displays down and project work to chuck away and people to say goodbye to for ever.

Yesterday I had my last session with counsellor-lady. First thing she said to me was, 'Goodness, you've shot up, Jolene!' That's because she hasn't seen me for months now I don't need her anger-management talks as much. 'So, are you looking forward to secondary school?' counsellor-lady asked. 'You're going to The Angel of the North Community College, aren't you? That's a long way to travel.'

Instead of mumbling an answer like I used to

do, I sat up straight and put a bit of feeling into it. 'Way-ay, man, I am going to the Angel! I can't wait, cos they've got a decent girls' football team and an all-weather pitch and a cracking sports hall . . .'

She smiled and nodded as I reeled off the list of sports facilities at the new place, then she said exactly the same thing my teachers have been telling me for months. 'The main thing is it will be a fresh start, Jolene.'

'Yep,' I agreed.

'You can make sure the school notices you for all the right reasons, like Jolene Nevin, captain of the girls' football team instead of Jolene Nevin captain of fighting and flare-ups!'

'I know,' I said, 'except I'll be Jolene Birtley.'

Birtley is Darryl my step-dad's last name. Birtley's not exactly flashy as last names go but it's better than Nevin, any day.

Counsellor-lady scribbled something on her clipboard then looked up and grinned. 'Well, that is progress,' she said. 'A year ago you wouldn't even acknowledge Darryl existed, let alone take his name.'

I couldn't argue with that; she was spot-on. When my mam first got together with Darryl, I couldn't stand him but, well, he kind of grew on me. Now I think Darryl's a top bloke and I love him to bits.

'What about his two boys? Are you still finding them . . .' she glanced at her notes and smiled again, '. . . wet and whingy?'

'Wet and whingy? Did I say that? Nah! They're crackin' lads. Keith's nine now and really into cars big-time and Jack's seven and doing my head in watching *Peter Pan* on DVD every two minutes but no, I get on with them great. Really great.'

'And your mum? How are things with her?' counsellor-lady asks cautiously.

'Yeah, things are great with her and all!' I said, bending down and rummaging in my bag so counsellor-lady wouldn't see my eyes and know I was lying. I quickly found the box of Mr Kipling's almond slices I'd bought for her and stuck it under her nose. 'This is for you, miss, for all your help. It's not much but I'm saving up for a new Sunderland shirt and you know what a rip-off price they are. Sorry they're not wrapped; we ran out of paper.'

'Why, thank you all the same, Jolene,' she said, though she looked a bit puzzled at my choice.

'They're the nearest I could get to currant buns,' I explained. 'Do you remember, you told me to say a rhyme when I thought I was losing it and the sparks started flying and I chose "Five currant buns in a baker's shop"?  Well, we haven't got a baker's shop near us so I had to make do with those from the Co-op instead.'

Counsellor-lady laughed and put the box in her leather bag which was bulging with files. 'I'll treasure them for ever,' she said.

'I wouldn't,' I told her, 'the sell-by date's up the end of this week.'

Anyway, that was yesterday and today's the Leavers' Service and I'm due up on stage any second so I'd best be off.

Chapter Two

The best bit of the Leavers' Service was at the end when we were told we could join our families. I jumped straight off the stage, vaulted over an empty pushchair, and dodged round about twenty-five rows of chairs to get to mine, I did.

They were stood near the back, next to the refreshments. I knew Mam wouldn't be coming—she said it wasn't worth losing a day's holiday for—but there was Darryl, grinning away, with Keith and Jack either side of him, and next to Darryl were my grandad Jake and his wife Kiersten and their twelve-year-old daughter

Brody. Yes, I know that makes Brody my very young auntie. It's Grandad's second marriage, OK? We specialize in them in my family but if I went into all the ins-and-outs we'd be here all day. Anyway, point was, everyone was there I wanted to be there, all right?

'Y'al reet, bonny lass? You were great!' Darryl said as I flew towards him and wrapped my arms round his generous—OK, massive—belly.

'I know!' I laughed, dead pleased to see them all and surprising Grandad and Kiersten by hugging them, too. I wouldn't normally go in for that touchy-feely stuff but this was a special occasion and they had made an effort and come all the way from Wakefield which is a hundred miles from here.

I was hyper all the way home. Not only had I finished primary school for good but Jack, Keith, and me were going to spend five days at Kirkham Lodge, Grandad and Kiersten's place. It would have been longer if Grandad hadn't had to bring his holiday in America forward. Still, five days was better than nothing, especially as we'd be going to Brody's brilliant After School club while we were there. Unfortunately, Grandad Jake was taking Brody and Kiersten to the Lakes for the weekend first. If it had been up to me we'd have set off right now. Still, it gave us time to pack, I suppose. And for Mam to have twenty more rows with Darryl.

It was the rows I was thinking about when counsellor-lady asked how things were with Mam and I'd just said 'great'. Things weren't great at all; they were chronic. Mam started the minute she came home from work just as we were finishing off our dinner. 'Where's Dad?' she snapped.

'They had to book in to the hotel but they did invite us over later for a drink,' Darryl explained opening the cupboard to find a clean plate for her.

'Typical,' Mam said, leaning against the worktop and examining her long nails, 'can't hang on two minutes.'

'It has gone seven, pet. We thought you were coming home at five,' Darryl pointed out.

Mam fixed Darryl with a glare cold enough to freeze the nuts off a squirrel. 'Back at five? I wish! I can't leave the salon, just like that. *I've* got a job with responsibilities.' She tapped the bronze name badge, engraved with her name and rank (assistant manager), which was pinned to her white, body-hugging overall.

CLAIRE BIRTLEY
Assistant Manager

'So what was Queen Kiersten wearing today?' she asked me. 'Some little designer number that cost more than this house, I suppose.'

I shrugged and ran a finger round the rim of my plate to get up the last of the sauce. 'I don't know. I didn't really look.'

Without warning, Mam sprang forward, her arm like a lizard's tongue darting out for a fly, and slapped me hard across the head. 'Stop acting like a pig! How many times do I have to tell you about using a knife and fork?' she growled.

I pressed my lips together, careful not to show how much the blow stung, especially with Keith and Jack sitting opposite. They flinch every time she lays one on me.

Darryl placed the steaming plate of meatballs and creamed potatoes we'd all enjoyed at the spare setting and told Mam to sit down but the disgusted look she gave the food was enough for him to know she wouldn't be touching it. 'Are you being funny? You know I'm not doing carbs! I thought you said you'd do something healthy like a salad?' she complained.

Darryl sighed. 'I've made salads all week. We can't live just on rabbit food, can we?'

Mam stared pointedly at Darryl's belly. 'No, apparently not,' she said coldly. 'Anyway, it doesn't matter. I'll get something down town.'

'Down town?'

'Yeah. I'm going out with Mandy and Risa.'

'Again?' Darryl asked. It was the third time this week she'd been out with those two. She knew them from when she worked on a cruise ship when I was little. I'd had to live with my Nana Lynne and Grandad Martin, Mam's step-dad, back then. It wasn't what you'd call a good experience. Counsellor-lady told me a lot of my 'anger issues' stemmed from that time because I felt I had been abandoned but you don't want to know about stuff like that. I'm over it. End of.

Mam was getting herself really wound up. 'What do you mean "again"?' she snarled, watching Darryl as he took her plate away and scraped the food into the bin. 'What am I? A prisoner in my own home? And it is *my* home, remember. It's *my* name on the papers.'

'So you keep telling me,' Darryl muttered.

Mam seemed to expand then, like an airbed being pumped up. 'Oh, I do, do I? Well, just you listen to me, mate, because . . .'

It had started. I nodded at Jack and Keith and led them out of the kitchen and headed upstairs to my bedroom. 'OK, mushes,' I said, grabbing my football and bouncing it on the floor to try to drown out the shouting, 'who wants a story?'

'I do!' said Jack, jumping on to my bed.

'What about?'

'About when we go to Neverland and meet Peter Pan and the Lost Boys.'

I rolled my eyes at Keith who did the same in return. Neverland stories were all Jack ever asked for. Downstairs, a door banged and something smashed, making both lads shudder. I bounced my football harder and began my story. 'OK. One day in Neverland, Wendy, wearing her new Sunderland shirt . . .'

Chapter Three

Grandad Jake, Kiersten, and Brody arrived at teatime on Sunday to take us back to Wakefield with them. It was a tight fit getting six of us into Grandad Jake's car, top of the range, as Keith pointed out, or not. 'Don't do anything I wouldn't do,' I told Mam and Darryl as they stood stiffly by the kerbside to see us off. They'd barely spoken since the row on Friday night.

'Just make sure you mind your manners,' Mam said to me, flicking her eyes quickly at Kiersten.

'Course I will,' I said, doing a fake burp that made everyone inside the car laugh.

Darryl stepped forward and leaned in close to my side, his face a mixture of concern and unease. 'Look after the lads for me, Jolene, won't you?'

'How can you even ask me that?' I said. 'You know I will.'

He nodded briefly. 'You've got your mobile with you, pet, haven't you?'

'Yep. And Jack's *Peter Pan* DVD and Keith's *Fastcars Monthly*. All the basics.'

'Right then. Give us a call when you get there.'

'We will.'

Mam then muttered something about not having time to hang around all day and retreated into the house. Darryl didn't though. He stayed right on that kerbside, waving at us until we were out of sight. 'He'll be there when we get back, I bet,' I joked.

'I hope so,' Keith whispered.

Keith hardly said a word throughout the journey and neither did Jack. I don't know whether they were quiet because they were still overawed by the company or because they were already missing Darryl but I made up for it by chatting non-stop to Brody about After School club. I wanted to be filled in with *all* the details and launched straight in. 'So what's the theme?'

She flicked her long, curly red hair back and grinned. 'How did I guess this would be your first topic of conversation? OK, the theme is Scrapyard Sculptures. Mrs Fryston's been collecting a whole heap of junk for weeks now to make them. The entire mobile's like some kind of yard sale. I'm totally amazed nobody's broken their neck yet.'

'Oh,' I said. Last time it had been football and other outdoor games; much more up my street. But—you know—whatever.

'And you're sure Alex is going to be there?' I continued. Alex McCormack is one of the kids I met there. She's my best friend.

Brody nodded. 'For sure. She can't wait to see you. And you guys,' she added, smiling at Keith and Jack. They just stared back at her.

'Hey, I hope you lads aren't this quiet all week, you know. I'm relying on you to give me a bit of male support!' Grandad told them.

'They won't be quiet,' I said, 'don't you worry.'

Still, it wasn't until we had said goodnight to everyone and closed the door of the grand bedroom we were sharing, that the lads found their tongues again. Then they began talking over each other in excited whispers. 'This is the best house ever! It's like Mr and Mrs Darling's house in *Peter Pan* but even bigger!' Jack giggled.

'Why are the walls covered in wood and not wallpaper?' Keith asked, passing his hand across the oak panelling. 'And why . . .'

He started asking about everything he'd seen since we arrived. That's what Keith does; you think he's staring into space but he isn't. He never misses a thing; just stores everything up in his brain for when he needs it. I answered him best I could, but not being an expert on big houses, I made half of it up.

'It's all frightfully delightful!' Jack said, unloading his stuffed animals and arranging them across his pillow in this particular order he has. 'Jolene, I think you'd better make tonight's story extra special.'

'And include wooden walls,' Keith said, pulling his pyjamas on.

'Will do,' I said, thinking what I wouldn't be doing was including the words 'frightfully delightful'. Honest—I would have to get Jack off that Peter Pan and Wendy rubbish when we got back, I really would.

Chapter Four

We didn't arrive at After School club until really late the next morning. That was all Brody's fault. She took years to eat her pancakes during breakfast then years more to get dressed. If I didn't know better I'd have said she was dragging it out on purpose.

Finally, at well after ten, we pulled up outside the school gates. The first thing I noticed was they'd been changed. There was new metal fencing all around the entrance and a mean-looking steel gate in place of the old wooden one. 'The school's had a lot of break-ins lately,' Brody said when I mentioned it.

'Same near us,' I told her.

'It's nothing compared to our house, though; it's like a fortress since we got burgled. Did you notice? Lights, cameras, beams, alarms—the works! I mean, I know I was kind of shaken by it at the time but Jake went a little bit OTT if you ask me. Even the rabbit's got a panic button!'

Inside the barriers, though, it was all so familiar and my heart leapt. We're here! I thought. Bring it on! I quickened my pace as we crossed the school playground, leading the way round the back of the red-brick school to the edge of the field where I knew we'd find the After School club. 'It's smaller than I thought it would be,' Keith said as we approached the steps.

'Small is beautiful,' I quipped, leading the way.

Inside, Jack and Keith went back to being a pair of shy Marys, hiding behind me while Kiersten and Brody sorted out admission slips with Mrs Fryston. I didn't protest about Jack and Keith using me as a shield too much. I was feeling a bit shy myself, not that I'd ever admit it in public.

It was a lot busier than last time I'd been. The

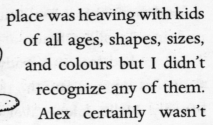

place was heaving with kids of all ages, shapes, sizes, and colours but I didn't recognize any of them. Alex certainly wasn't there, though her mam, one of the several helpers, was. Mrs McCormack was looking slightly hassled, as always, as she mopped up a spilt pot of paint from her crowded craft table by the window.

I knew Alex sometimes came later in the holidays depending on what time her sister Caitlin brought her so I tried not to worry too much but it was weird that I didn't know *anyone*. Lloyd or Reggie, Brody's boyfriend, or my old enemy Sammie Wesley or that Sam kid who sometimes spoke in rhymes or even little Brandon, who only missed if there was an emergency. Not one of them was here. I felt the first stab of uncertainty since we arrived. What if they'd all left and After School club was rubbish now?

'It's a bit noisy,' Jack whispered, clinging to my hand.

21

'And that's before our Keith gets going!' I joked, nudging the silent figure at my side.

He looked lost and ready to do a runner, but then Mrs Fryston saw the three of us and smiled broadly. 'Hello, Jolene. Welcome back. Goodness, you've shot up!' she said.

'People keep telling me that!' I replied.

'And this is Keith and Jack?' she asked, coming over and kneeling down so she was eye level with them.

They stared numbly back at her from behind me. 'Yeah. They're a bit quiet, like, but they'll join in when they're ready.'

'Perhaps they'd like to have a walk round with me, so I can show them what we're doing today?' Mrs Fryston suggested.

I expected them to shake their heads and refuse but I'd forgotten how everyone trusts Mrs Fryston from the start. They disappeared then, over to the far side of the mobile which had been sectioned off with bookcases.

'Well, that's them sorted, what do you want to do?' Brody asked, coming to stand next to me after she'd waved goodbye to Kiersten.

'I don't know,' I said, shrugging my shoulders. 'What is there?'

She stretched her arms out and did this massive yawn. 'Ooh, I don't know about you but I could do with some fresh air. That early start has kind of knocked me out. Do you wanna take a walk round the Patch?'

'The Patch?'

'It's a new thing—a joint venture the school and the After School club are working on. You know where the caretaker's bungalow used to be?'

I nodded, though I didn't really.

'Well, she's been upgraded to a more modern place and they've knocked the old bungalow down and used the land for a kind of wildlife area known as The Patch. It's where we're going to put all the sculptures when they're finished. Come on, I'll show you.'

'OK,' I said, following Brody out reluctantly. The Patch. It sounded well boring.

Chapter Five

At the far end of the field behind the school and what felt like miles across from the mobile was another fenced-in area. The fencing was quite high—reaching the top of my head—but instead of being  made of wire mesh, this time it was made of long, slanted thick twigs you couldn't see through. 'Willow,' Brody said, stepping through a gate at the side, 'isn't it lovely?'

'If you say so,' I mumbled.

Inside wasn't that much to write home about, either. Just a big square area the size of a tennis court filled with lots of puny-looking plants propped up with bamboo canes. Down the centre ran a winding pathway leading to what looked like a tepee made out of more twigs. The tepee-thing dominated the area, rising high above everything, including the fence, but it still didn't impress me much.

'It's a work in progress,' Brody said, seeing my long face. 'In a couple of years there'll be trees and all kinds of plants in here and maybe a pond. It's a shame I shan't be around to see it. Wanna go sit in the den?'

'Not really,' I said glumly, 'I'd rather go check on our Keith and Jack.'

'Oh, they'll be fine. Come on.' Brody grabbed my hand and pulled me along the path towards the 'den'. 'The Year Sixes at the school built it,' she said, her voice getting louder as we approached the heap, 'some feat of engineering, huh?'

'Mm,' I said, unconvinced.

'Try the door; it's really clever. They've made like a latch so it opens and closes properly. I think Sam and Sammie worked on that part.'

'Great,' I said, flicking up a nub of varnished wood that jutted from a roughly sawn hole in the door. The door, which only came chest high, sprang open instantly, revealing nothing but darkness.

'Go in,' Brody urged.

'OK,' I sighed, crouching and thinking 'what for?' but as soon as I set foot inside I got a right shock. There were yells of 'surprise!' and what felt like dozens of hands grabbing hold of me.

'Jo-lene, Jo-lene, Jo-lene, Jo-le-e-ene!' everyone sang, almost in tune, to the song my name came from. I still couldn't make out who was there but light suddenly appeared as someone rolled up what must have been a blind to reveal a kind of window—if you can call it that, the frame was pretty wonky—and there they all were. Reggie in his goofy specs, Sam Riley with his tidy, blond hair, chunky Sammie Wesley grinning like a cat, little Brandon, dressed in his army combats, Lloyd looking scruffy in his muddy jeans and baggy jumper, and, of course, Alex. Alex, her chestnut hair shining as the sun caught it from behind, had this huge grin on her face and I knew that grin was just for me. One by one they all let go except for her. 'Hello,' Alex said, still squeezing the life out of me, 'what took you?'

Poor Darryl couldn't get a word in edgeways when he phoned that night. The three of us kept passing the phone from one to the other, each telling him something of the day while another one added bits from behind. 'And I played with Brandon nearly all the time,' Jack said. 'He's funny, like Tootles.'

'Tell him about Ruby trying to give the hamster a high-five with her Barbie doll,' Keith whispered.

'And tell him about the trip tomorrow,' I added to that.

Tomorrow, to kick off the summer theme of 'Scrapyard Sculptures' Mrs Fryston had organized a coach to take us to a place called the Yorkshire Sculpture Park which was just outside Wakefield. Apparently it was full of all these sculptures and works of art from famous people dotted about in the open.

'Dad wants to talk to you now,' Jack said, handing the phone over to me.

'About time! You've hogged it for long enough!' I told him. He stuck his tongue out and went to join Keith and Brody in the living room. 'Haway, Darryl, how are you?' I asked.

'I'm fine, pet, and I can tell from your voice and the lads that you all are, too.'

'Oh, yeah. They're loving it!'

'That's good to know, good to know.'

His voice sounded relieved but a bit flat, too. 'What about at home? How's it going with Mam? Is she there? Can I talk to her?'

'Oh, er . . . she's not in at the minute.'

'Don't tell me she's out again.'

'I don't know where she is, to be honest.'

'Well, when she gets back will you tell her I said hello.'

He hesitated for ages before replying. 'Sure I will. Listen, look after the lads for me, won't you?'

'Will you stop asking me that? I told you when we left I'd look after them, didn't I? Flipping heck, man!'

He laughed then, thank goodness. 'Goodnight, Jolene, pet. Sleep tight.'

'You too.'

Aw. I don't want to sound all mushy, but you've got to admit Darryl's just the perfect dad, isn't he?

Chapter Six

Next morning, Kiersten dropped us off in the car park. Brody wasn't with us because she needed to pack for her holidays so Kiersten said she'd wait with us until the coach arrived if we wanted but there was no need. As soon as we got there, Jack and Keith disappeared to be with their mates and I settled down to be with mine, Alex. 'You're like a bunch of old timers,' Kiersten smiled as she drove away.

When the coach came, everyone cheered but no one was allowed on until Mrs Fryston had registered us and done a triple head count and

given everyone a lecture about best behaviour and sticking with our group leaders. There were about twenty-five kids and eight leaders, including Caitlin, Alex's sister, who is one of the holiday staff, and her boyfriend Simon. Jack, Brandon, Ruby, Alex, and me were in Mrs Fryston's group. Keith had joined Lloyd and Reggie and Sam in Caitlin's. Alex was a bit grumpy because she wanted us to be with Caitlin but I pointed out I had to stick with Jack anyway so she was OK then.

The journey only took about forty minutes. I couldn't believe it when Alex told me we were already there. Usually I'm halfway through my lunch by the time I reach my destination on a school trip but I hadn't even had a chance to open my sandwiches before the coach was turning into a gateway bounded by a low drystone wall and signposted 'Yorkshire Sculpture Park'.

'This is it,' Alex said as the coach trundled slowly down a narrow winding road with hills and trees stretching into the distance. Scattered about the fields were all sorts of sculptures: black marble women with holes through their heads; tall, thin metal contraptions; and squat, round objects big enough to climb through. Nothing struck me as being as impressive as the Angel of the North up near us in Gateshead, though. They'd have to go some to beat that. I mean, even my new school had been named after it.

When we jumped down from the coach, Mrs Fryston gave one member from each group a disposable camera so we could take pictures of the sculptures. Alex was in charge of ours and took loads of our favourite: a tall bloke with his arms by his sides painted in a streaky orange. 'Tango Man' we called him.

When we all met up for lunch, Reggie got told off because he'd used all his group's film up on taking snaps of cowpats and sheep droppings and, for once, the others complained about him. When Mrs Fryston asked him why, Reggie just shrugged. 'If that bloke can get away with sawing a shark in half, then a cowpat's a work of art in my book,' he said.

Quick as a flash, our Keith replied, 'That's one book I won't be getting out of the library!' I felt dead proud of him for making everybody laugh. I couldn't wait to tell Darryl how well Keith and Jack were settling in but when Kiersten picked us up she said he'd called already to let us know he had to work overtime and wouldn't be home until after our bedtime. Never mind, I thought, it will keep.

Do you know, I slept like a log that night because of all that fresh air—no, two logs—no, three!

Chapter Seven

Wednesday already—the week was racing away. Today, we actually got down to planning and designing our sculptures that would eventually end up on display in the Patch. Pity I wouldn't be around to see that part but at least I could make a start.

Jack wanted to make his sculpture with Brandon and Keith wanted to do one with Lloyd. All that was fine by me. A: it meant they were settling in, B: it meant I could have some one-on-one time with Alex. We found ourselves a place to work away from everyone else so we could have some peace. 'Did I show you this?' Alex said, sliding a flat brown paper bag towards me.

'What is it?'

'Have a look. I bought it in the shop yesterday.'

I slid out the postcard, which was a picture of that orange sculpture we'd both liked. 'Tango Man!' I said.

'Yeah, but look who it's by.'

I flipped over to read the writing. '"One and Other" by Antony Gormley! He did the Angel of the North! No wonder we liked this one best. He's the man, he is.'

Alex grinned and pulled me over to the window. 'Look what I baggied last night when everybody had gone home,' she whispered, and pulled the curtain back to show me an old tailor's dummy.

'Perfect!' I said.

'Except the head's missing.'

'No problem. We don't want to copy Tango Man exactly, do we? We'll call it . . . Headless Herbert.'

'And paint it yellow instead of orange.'

'Exactly.'

'Let's get going then!' she said.

We spent all day covering Headless Herbert in mod rock so the paint wouldn't just sink into the fabric. That was Alex's idea; she's clever like that. It was really good, too; everyone who passed told us so.

While we made our sculpture, Alex and I just talked and talked, not even bothering to stop for lunch. It was as if we knew we had to get a term's worth of nattering in before I went back to Washington. We talked about ordinary stuff, like how I felt about moving to a new school and how she felt about going into Year Six. She said she was worried about doing the SATs and I told her not to be because they were a piece of cake. When we were sure no one was listening, we got more personal. I asked her what was happening with her brother Daniel's grave. He was only four when he died and his ashes have been stuck on their mantelpiece for, like, twelve years or something, but they were getting a proper grave now. 'It's all arranged,' Alex said, 'the headstone's nearly ready and we're going to have a family service for him in early August. The nice thing is he'll be quite close to Grandma's plot.'

'That's mint,' I said, 'he'll have someone to talk to.'

'Yeah.' She took another layer of mod rock and soaked it in water. 'I'll miss him, though. Is that weird, do you think? Missing someone's ashes?'

'No. Why is it? I mean, it's still your brother, isn't it? I'd be just the same if anything happened to Keith or Jack.'

'Would you?'

'Course.'

'That's nice. It shows how much you love them, even though they're not your real brothers, if you know what I mean.'

'Yeah, I do know what you mean but I don't see what difference that makes. I know loads of people with real brothers and they hate their guts.'

'That's true!' Alex laughed.

I glanced round quickly, to check my lads were OK. Jack was sticking a kitchen roll tube to a cardboard box, concentrating so hard his tongue was sticking out. Keith was hunched over a large sheet of paper, pointing things out to Lloyd who nodded and then bent to add something with his pencil. Keith must have felt me staring at him then because he looked up and smiled. I stuck my thumb up at him and winked. No, if anything happened to either Keith or Jack, I'd be gutted.

'Will they go to the same high school as you when they're old enough?' Alex asked. 'I'm going to the same one as Caitlin.'

'Yeah, I hope so. Eh, did I tell you about the sports facilities?'

'Yeah, about a million times.'

'What, even the all-weather pitch?'

'Two million times.'

I laughed and so did she. For some reason, we kept laughing, and couldn't stop. My stomach was killing me in the end. When Mrs

Fryston came across to see what the racket was, she shook her head and smiled. 'That's what I like to see. Best friends having a good time.'

Chapter Eight

After the club had finished, Grandad Jake picked us up and drove straight to Piccollino's, an Italian restaurant near the station where I'd been before. Brody and Kiersten were already waiting outside, sussing out the specials on the blackboard. 'I just didn't feel like cooking,' Kiersten explained as she pushed open the glass door to go in. 'Besides, I'm trying to run the fridge down. I don't want things rotting in there while we're away.' They were travelling to Heathrow first thing Saturday morning, so it made sense.

It was fun, that meal. I was so chilled out from

being with Alex all afternoon I didn't have much more to say. That didn't matter, though. I was happy just watching and listening to everyone else. Brody made us all laugh by talking about her aunties in Topeka they would be staying with and how 'ditzy' they all were. Jack made *me* laugh by just staring at Brody, all goofy, as she talked. I think Reggie had better watch out—he had competition there. Keith surprised me the most, waving his arms about all over the place at us about his sculpture and how he and Lloyd had spent most of their time walking round the Patch, working out where would be the best position for it. 'We thought next to the den but then it won't catch the light there so we're now thinking near the fence so it gets a striped effect when the sun shines on it.'

'That's real artistic thinking,' Kiersten complimented him.

'Oh,' he said, blushing.

'Well, Keith, laddo, you've certainly bucked up since you arrived!' Grandad told him which is just what I'd been thinking. I wasn't the only one who changed when they got to Brody's After School club.

We were all full after the main course and none of us wanted a pudding so we were back at the house by half past seven. Brody put her new CD on and we were all singing along to that when we pulled into the drive.

'Whose is that?' Grandad asked as he had to pull up behind a car blocking his way. 'Are we expecting anyone, Kierst?'

'That's Dad!' Keith announced before she could reply.

Chapter Nine

After the excitement of seeing Darryl on the doorstep, we all went inside but once he'd sat down and I looked at him properly, I knew something was wrong. He looked terrible; he hadn't shaved, his shirt was all creased and not even buttoned up properly, and he couldn't sit still. One second he was leaning back against the cushions on the settee, one leg bouncing up and down restlessly, the next he was hunched forward, his knees pressed into the low coffee table in front of him. I sighed and came right out with it. 'What's Mam done now?' I asked him.

He let out this fake laugh and said, 'Oh, nothing, nothing.'

Like I believed that.

I got up and planted myself right in front of him, folding my arms across my chest so he knew I meant business. 'What's going on, Darryl? Tell me,' I said.

'Jolene,' Grandad said, 'let the poor guy have his tea.'

'It's all right, Jake, Jolene's right, something's cropped up,' Darryl replied, not looking at me.

'Such as?' I asked, not budging. Bad news is best delivered quick, I reckon.

Darryl cleared his throat a couple of times before answering. 'Well, it's like this,' he began, then stopped, glanced up at me for a second, shook his head and mumbled.

'What?'

'Their nan's sick. She was taken into hospital . . .' he said, trailing off, too cut up to continue.

There was an outbreak of 'oh nos' and 'I'm

sorrys' from everyone, including me. I felt like a proper toe-rag then. There was me acting all bolshy and making Darryl come right out with his bad news in front of everyone when he'd probably been saving it until he had us in private. I liked their nan, too. She was called Pam and she was a warden in an old people's complex and she always let me choose her lottery numbers for her.

'What's wrong with her?' Keith asked, his eyes brimming with tears. 'Is she going to die?'

'No! No!' Darryl said in alarm, his face turning beetroot. 'But the sooner we set off, the sooner we get to see her, yeah?'

Keith nodded and took Jack's hand. 'We'll go get our stuff,' he said, his voice all choked.

'Yeah,' I said, patting Darryl on the shoulder before I went, 'we won't be long.' It was a bummer I'd miss out on the last two days with Alex and wouldn't get to finish Headless Herbert with her but family comes first, right?

I turned to follow Jack and Keith upstairs but Darryl stood up then, nearly sending all the tea things flying. 'Jolene, no,' he said, his voice low but sharp, 'it's just the lads. You stay here. Your mam's coming for you on Friday as planned. No point you cutting your holiday short, is there?'

'But I want to . . .'

'Please, pet,' he said, more softly this time, 'it's less complicated this way.'

Chapter Ten

Next day felt funny without Jack and Keith at After School club. Everyone was sympathetic but Lloyd and Brandon were the most disappointed. 'Oh, but I needed Keith to choose the final design for our sculpture,' Lloyd said, scratching the back of his neck.

'I'll ask him tonight when I talk to him,' I promised.

'Jack was going to play with me,' Brandon pouted.

'I'll tell him you asked after him when I phone,' I promised again.

Trouble was, nobody answered when I called the house. The phone just rang and rang. Neither Darryl or Mam returned my texts, either, but Grandad Jake told me he didn't think mobile phones were allowed to be switched on in hospital wards. They mess up the heart monitors or something.

It was about half nine when Mam finally picked up the phone at home. 'Hello?' she answered, her voice all croaky and choked up.

'Hi, it's me,' I said.

'Oh, Jolene,' she sobbed.

'What's wrong? Is it Pam?'

'What?'

'Pam. Is it bad?'

'What are you talking about?'

'P-a-m. Pam, Darryl's mam. The one that's really ill in hospital, remember!'

'Oh, that's what he told you, is it?' She laughed but it turned into a snort then another sob.

'What do you mean?' I asked.

Mam took a deep breath. 'He's left me, Jolene. He's left me—wants a divorce as soon as possible.'

I suppose I should have felt shocked but I didn't. The news wasn't exactly unexpected. How could it be, the way they'd been hammering on when I left? Mam went on and on about what a useless husband Darryl had been, especially after all she had done for him. 'How dare he leave me, the big lump!' she ended.

'I've no idea, Mam. It's a mystery,' I said, then checked what time she'd be coming for me.

'Mid-morning and you'd better be ready. I've got to work late.'

'Great,' I said and hung up.

Being picked up mid-morning meant I didn't have time to go to After School club the next day. I called Alex's house first thing and told her why. 'Oh, Jolene, I'm really sorry,' she said, sounding all upset.

'Forget it,' I replied, 'I'm not bothered. It's not

like it's a total shock or anything. Sorry about dumping you with Headless Herbert on your own.'

'It's OK. I'll send you a picture of him when he's finished.'

'That'd be mint.'

There was a pause and I could almost feel her frowning through the telephone wires. 'Are you sure you're OK, Jolene?' she asked.

'What do you mean?'

'It's just you sound way too calm. If my parents had split up I'd be crying my eyes out.'

'Yeah, but your parents actually like each other!'

'I guess. What about Keith and Jack? You're going to really miss them, aren't you?'

'Why?'

She hesitated, thinking she'd said the wrong thing. 'Well . . . er . . . you won't see them as much, will you?'

'Yeah, course I will. I'll be seeing them every day, seeing as I'll be living with them!'

'Oh,' Alex said, sounding surprised, 'I thought you'd be with your mum.'

I nearly started choking when she said that. 'Eh? What would I want to live with my mam for? Darryl's much better at bringing kids up—he's a natural. My mam's rubbish—she's the first to admit it. She left me to live with my nan for four years once, remember.'

'I know but she's still your mum . . .' Alex began but I interrupted her. I wanted her to get this straight from the start because living with my mam instead of Darryl was not—repeat *not*—an option. 'Look, who's the one who turns up for Leavers' Services and parents' evenings? Darryl. Who asks me what sort of day I've had and if I'm OK as soon as I walk in? Darryl. Who never shouts at me or slaps me round the head? Darryl. Do you get what I'm saying or do you want more examples?'

'OK, OK, don't get your knickers in a twist; I was only asking! I just thought your mum might have wanted you to stay with her. She'll be all alone, won't she?'

'Yeah! For about two seconds until she finds a new boyfriend!'

'She might not.'

I was going to laugh but I stopped myself. Alex only saw the good side of people and I didn't want her to think I was being cruel. It's just I knew what Mam was like, that's all. If Alex had been let down by her mam as often as I'd been let down by mine, she'd be reacting the same way as I was now. 'I'll probably see Mam at weekends,' I said instead.

Alex didn't say anything for a few seconds; I could tell she was having trouble taking it all in. Her world and mine were so different sometimes. 'Oh . . . well . . . let me know your new address, won't you?' she said.

'Definitely. I'll let you know it as soon as I find out myself. It probably won't be a massive house or anything but who cares as long as we're together, right?'

'Right! Oh, good luck with everything, Jolene.'

'Ta!'

'I am sorry.'

'Well you don't have to be! It's not your fault,

you daft nit! Anyway, I'd better go. Talk to you soon, Alex.'

'Hope so.'

'Know so!'

Chapter Eleven

When Mam arrived, all puffy-eyed, she wouldn't even stay for a coffee. 'Can't,' she told Grandad Jake when he asked, 'I get too weepy when I just sit—I need to be on the move and doing things.' It didn't stop her sneaking a long look at what Kiersten was wearing from under her eyelids when she thought no one was watching, though. You see, I know what she's like. Those tears would dry up faster than a puddle in a desert as soon as we got outside.

I was glad Mam wanted a quick getaway, though. I don't like long goodbyes, either, and the sooner we got home, the sooner I could start packing. Brody nearly crushed my ribs with her hug and said she was missing me already, Grandad handed me twenty pounds for 'things' for my new school, and Kiersten said that I was welcome to 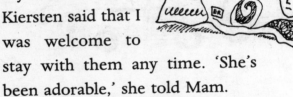 stay with them any time. 'She's been adorable,' she told Mam.

Mam frowned. 'Adorable? Our Jolene?'

In the car, Mam did nothing but moan all the way to the motorway. 'So, they're off to America for a month in the morning. Huh! It's all right for some.' It was no use telling Mam it wasn't really a holiday, just a long round of visiting relatives. I leaned forward to switch on the radio but she told me to switch it off again. 'I've got a headache,' she said. 'Anyway, I want to talk to you.'

'What about?'

'What about? The weather, of course! Honestly!

What do you think about?' she snapped, pulling into the outside lane of the A1 carriageway to overtake a row of northbound lorries.

'OK,' I said, 'talk.'

After all that she didn't say anything for a minute, just kept on overtaking in the outside lane, a deep scowl on her face. Eventually, she glanced sideways at me, biting her lip. 'Jolene, I'm going to be straight with you because that's how you and me are, right? Straight with each other? No beating about the bush?'

'I suppose.'

'Well, now Darryl's gone, things are going to get a bit tight financially . . .'

'Mmm.'

'And while I love my job it doesn't pay enough

to keep the mortgage going on my own but there's no way I'm selling my house.'

'OK.'

'That's our future in that house and I've worked my fingers to the bone for it.'

'OK,' I said, hoping the whole conversation wasn't going to be as boring as this. Mam took a deep breath and came to the point.

'Well . . . there's a job going . . .'

'Yeah?'

'. . . on the *Belle Helene* . . .'

'Mandy's boat?'

She nodded and began talking really fast as if her life depended upon it. 'The Tropical Paradise Tour. I'm thinking about applying but I wanted to run it by you first. See how you felt. It'd only be six months away but . . . it means I could rent the house out and that would sort the mortgage for a bit . . . plus I'd be earning. You get amazing tips on the cruises; so many rich old biddies wanting treatments and paying top whack for them . . .'

'Go for it,' I said.

She almost steered into the crash barrier when she heard that. 'Really?'

'Yeah, why not?'

'I thought you'd be mad at me.'

'Why should I be?'

She laughed nervously. 'Well, it'd mean you living with Nana and Grandad Martin and going to a different high school.'

I laughed then. 'Yeah, as if!'

'What do you mean "as if"?'

'As if I'll be at Nana's when I'll be with Darryl.'

'Eh? No you won't.'

'Course I will.'

She gave an empty, howling laugh then when she realized I was being serious. 'So that's why you've been so laid-back about everything? You think you're going to live with that big lump?'

'He's called Darryl,' I said through gritted teeth.

'Well, think again! He won't have you.'

'Yeah, whatever.'

Mam concentrated on the road for a minute, a deep scowl on her face. 'I'm telling you for a fact he won't.'

'Whatever.'

She glanced at me, her face set hard. 'Well, that's brilliant, that is! That makes me feel wonderful. Here I am, heartbroken, looking for a bit of support and what do I get? My own daughter doesn't even want to live with me. She just instantly presumes she's going to live with some bloke she's not even related to.'

'He's not some bloke. You were married to him!'

'So?'

'So talk sense.'

Mam was getting madder and madder. 'Don't tell me to talk sense! Ooh! I knew you'd come back from that place full of it.'

I sighed. I didn't want an argument about Grandad and Kiersten. I just wanted to get back to Washington. 'I don't get why you're kicking up a fuss about me living with Darryl. You've just told me I won't *be* living with you, haven't you? You'll be in a tropical paradise, so what difference does it make?'

Mam took her left hand off the steering wheel

and slammed me so hard I'd have dinted the door if I hadn't been wearing a seatbelt. 'How many more times?' she yelled at me. 'He won't have you! I wish he would! You deserve each other!'

'All you have to do is drop me off there!' I bellowed right back at her.

'Fine,' Mam snarled, pushing her foot down on the accelerator, 'I'll drop you off there. Let's see what happens, shall we?'

'Yeah,' I said, looking straight ahead, my hands shaking from the argument, 'let's.'

Chapter Twelve

Neither of us spoke again until we were on the outskirts of Washington, when Mam turned right on to the Armstrong Industrial estate, then did an emergency stop outside Crossley and Singh's, the big do-it-yourself store and builder's merchants where Darryl worked. 'Right then,' she said.

'Right then what?'

'You don't believe me? Go ask him for yourself. Go on, go ask him.'

I frowned at her but she just pulled down the vanity

mirror in the car sunshield and began to put lipstick on.

'Now? I don't want to now,' I said, less certain than I had been. The long silence had given me time to think; time to wonder why Darryl hadn't just taken me back with him the other day when he'd picked up the lads. Time to admit Mam might just be telling the truth and that he actually didn't want me. Mam might be a lot of things but she didn't usually lie about stuff. 'He might not be there,' I said, trying not to show how uncertain I felt.

'He'll be there and I'll be here. Waiting.'

She said it so cockily I wanted to knock the lipstick out of her hand and scribble over her silly face with it. 'Don't bother,' I told her, snatching my backpack instead, 'I'll probably go straight home with him.'

'I'll wait all the same,' she said.

'Please yourself,' I told her, leaping out of the car. If she wanted to waste her time, that was up to her.

I hurried through the automatic glass entrance door but I knew I wouldn't be allowed to continue through into the loading bays so I had to ask the bloke on the help desk to send out a message over the tannoy system for Darryl. I felt dead important when they announced 'Will Darryl Birtley please report to the enquiries desk as he has a visitor.'

Darryl, wearing a tangerine coloured boiler-suit and wiping his hands on a grimy cloth, approached the desk with a puzzled look on his face. When he saw me, the look changed to confusion. 'Haway, pet. What are you doing here? You're not alone, are you?' he asked nervously, looking round.

I couldn't answer at first, I was just so pleased to see him. Forgetting all the nasty things Mam had said, I hugged him and told him I'd come straight here after Mam had picked me up from Grandad Jake's. 'Oh,' he said, sounding embarrassed.

I didn't want to make him feel bad by reminding him he'd fibbed about Pam so I rattled on about the journey and Headless Herbert and other rubbish for a few minutes instead. 'Anyway, here

I am, Trouble United! What time do you finish? Shall I just wait for you or what?'

Darryl glanced up at the help desk bloke and steered me towards the display of garden benches nearby. 'What do you mean, pet?'

'Shall I just hang round here—you know—until it's time for you to take me home with you? I can pick up all my clothes and stuff tomorrow. I just want to come back with you and see the lads now.'

A shadow crossed his face. 'I can't take you home with me, Jolene.'

'Why not?' I asked. I tried to keep my voice steady. There'd be a dead simple reason. Overtime, bet you.

He slumped down on one of the benches and I slumped next to him. 'Well, I haven't got a home, to start with. The lads are at their mam's and I'm at my mam's until I get sorted out.'

I let this news sink in for a second. It wasn't great news but it wasn't a disaster, was it? Darryl hadn't said he didn't want me, only that things were tough at the moment. 'How long do you think it'll be until you are sorted?' I asked him.

He ran his hand roughly over his prickly hair. 'Weeks, months, who knows? It depends on what the solicitors have to say . . . I saw them this morning . . . it wasn't . . .'

'Wasn't what?' I asked him when he didn't finish his sentence.

He looked at me, then quickly looked at his feet, shaking his head. 'It wasn't good.'

I shrugged. Solicitors didn't mean much to me; I didn't know or care what they did. All I needed to know, really, really needed to know, was when I could move in with Darryl. I leaned over and nudged his arm, looking up at the ceiling as if to say, 'What a pain, eh?'

'I suppose I could go back to Mam's for a bit but try and get fixed up before I start at the Angel, won't you, mush? I don't want to miss the trials for the girls' footy team.' I said it in a light, jokey way but he knew I meant it.

All the colour drained from Darryl's face but he just shook his head. 'Jolene, you can't live with me, pet, not ever.'

I gave him a wonky smile. I hadn't heard him properly. 'What?'

'You can't live with me . . . with us. I'm not . . . I'm not your proper dad.'

Well, we all knew that. My so-called 'proper' dad had done a runner before I'd even been born. What had that got to do with it? I laughed. It came out sounding fake, even to me. 'So? Who cares about that? You're like a proper dad so that's all that matters, isn't it? It's like I said to Alex the other day when she was talking about Jack and Keith not being my real brothers . . .'

I repeated the conversation I'd had with Alex and waited for him to nod and say, 'Course it is, pet. I don't know what I'm on about!' But he didn't. He just began shaking his head as he backed up to the corner of the bench, away from me. 'No,' he said, 'no, no, no. Don't do this to me, pet. I'm worried enough about having to leave Jack and Keith with Tracie. It took me that long to get custody of them in the first place. I can't worry about you, too.'

I stared at him for a minute, thinking why?

Why couldn't he worry about me too? Because if he didn't worry about me, it meant Mam hadn't been telling fibs in the car. It meant he didn't want me. And if he didn't want me, it would break my heart. 'Darryl,' I said, reaching out my hand to touch him, but he jumped up as if he'd spilt hot tea down his overalls.

'No, Jolene,' he said, wincing, 'I can't do this. Go home. Go to your mam.'

And he stalked off without looking back at all. The big lump.

Mam took one look at my face as I flung myself into the front seat next to her and twisted the key in the ignition with a flourish. 'Told you,' she said.

Chapter Thirteen

I stayed in my bedroom all weekend, barring the door and screaming at Mam to bleep-bleep off every time she came near. 'Suit yourself, Jolene,' she said in the end, 'I've got better things to do than waste time on your moods.'

On Saturday night, when I knew Mam was asleep, I sneaked downstairs to get something to eat. 'Like a midnight feast in Neverland,' I imagined Jack whispering. Jack and Keith. Where were they tonight? I wondered what fibs Darryl had told *them* on the journey home? Did they know they wouldn't be living with me again?

Would maybe never see me again? Because that's what happened. I'd talked to enough kids at school whose parents had split to know the score. It started off with weekend visits, if you were lucky, then every other weekend, then now and again in the holidays, then maybe some other time . . . then nothing. Huh! I hadn't even started off with weekend visits, had I? I'd gone straight to nothing.

I opened the fridge door but instead of seeing cheese and salad, I just saw Darryl's stupid face. 'I'm not your proper dad. I can't worry about *you*, Jolene!' it sneered. I slammed the fridge door shut and dashed back upstairs.

I didn't think of a comeback until I was on the dark landing. *Well, just because you don't want me, it doesn't mean the lads don't!*

Yeah, Dad. Just because you don't want her doesn't mean we don't! their voices echoed in support.

I stopped by their old bedroom, laying my head on the smooth paintwork for a second. I missed them so much already. Turning the handle carefully so Mam wouldn't wake, I tiptoed into their room, just to feel nearer to them. Maybe I'd sleep on one of their beds, or maybe I'd find something of theirs I could keep under my pillow, as a memento.

It was a mistake, going in there. A big mistake. Even though I hadn't turned on the light, the moon was shining so clearly through the curtainless window, what I saw really shocked and hurt me, like a mis-kicked ball in the guts or one of Mam's unexpected back-handers. Smack—take that!

Their room had been stripped bare. All their furniture, curtains, toys, games, everything. There wasn't even a pair of socks left to remind me who'd once lived here. Not a thing. Mam had scrubbed Jack and Keith out of her life just like Darryl had scrubbed me out of his.

Grown-ups. They made me sick.

I spent the rest of the night staring out of my bedroom window, trying to send signals to Jack and Keith miles away at their mam's, wherever that was, to let them know I wouldn't forget them, ever.

'Do you want a story?' I whispered.

Chapter Fourteen

On Monday morning, Mam rapped sharply on my door and told me she was going to work. 'I want you up and dressed by the time I come home or else, Jolene! Enough is enough!'

She was right. Enough was enough and I'd *had* enough—of her, of Darryl, of the lot of them. The second I heard her car roar away, I threw back my duvet, headed for the bathroom, took a shower, had a sniff at my Sunderland shirt and decided it was minging, chucked it in the laundry basket and put on my clean replica away-shirt instead.

Downstairs, I made a pot of tea and some toast. My backpack was still on the chair where I'd flung it, unopened. That was good—it would save a bit of time on the packing. I began rummaging about in the fridge; I'd need food to take with me. Kiersten had said she was trying to get rid of all her fresh food. No point arriving at Grandad Jake's with nothing to eat. That'd be daft.

Back to Grandad Jake's; that's where I was going today. I wasn't going to hang around here until Mam decided to bunk off on her cruise ships. I knew her. Six months would turn into six years; she'd done it before and she'd do it again. Well, stuff that for a game of soldiers. I wasn't going to live with Nana Lynne and Grandad Martin again. She was always sozzled and he was always nasty. I'd have no arms left by the time he'd finished pinching and nipping them. Stay with them, Mam? You're having a laugh.

I'd go to the one place I've always been made to feel welcome. What was it Kiersten had said before I left? You're welcome here any time, Jolene? Well, any time had come. All I had to do was lie low for a month until they returned from Topeka.

It was a cinch getting on the train at Newcastle. I just told the woman at the counter that my dad was parking the car when she asked if I was unaccompanied. Then when she asked why we didn't get our tickets at the same time I thought of Grandad Jake and said, 'Dad's already got a season ticket, he's a commuter,' and that was that. Mission accomplished.

It was only lunchtime, so I found an empty seat easily enough and stared out of the window the whole journey, remembering this time last year. I had run away from home then, too. Mam had arranged to go on holiday without me and I was meant to stay at Grandad Martin and Nana's. No change there, then. I don't know why she always dumped me with them when she knew they were useless and I hated them. 'They're the only ones that will have you,' she always said when I asked her. Was that true? Was that why Darryl had been so quick to get rid of me? I was too much trouble? Get over it, Jolene, I growled to myself. What did I care? I was Jolene Nevin, captain of fights and flare-ups, me. I didn't need anybody.

I crunched into my apple, and planned what to do when I got to Grandad Jake's house. Take a shower in their posh en suite? Make myself some of those golden pancakes Brody loved? Watch a bit of telly? I'd check out the Sunderland website on the Internet, too, to see if we'd bought any new players. Easy life, Jolene, I thought, snuggling right down in my seat. 'Girl, you are a genius!'

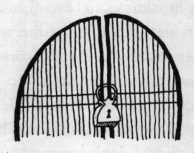

It was when I stood outside Kirkham Lodge, three hours later, staring at the electronic gates that were normally open but were now fastened and padlocked, I realized I might not be such a genius after all. I'd forgotten one or two things about what people do when they go on holiday. Things like cancelling the milk and shutting the house up good and proper. At Kirkham Lodge it wasn't like we were talking about making sure the door was locked, either. Brody hadn't been exaggerating that day she told me about the burglar alarms; we really were talking sensors, floodlights, and cameras.

I glanced up at the high sandstone wall on either side of the gates and knew I had no chance of getting into the house. I'd be busted the second I touched the front door, if I even got that far without being electrocuted or something. Bogger. Bogger, bogger, bogger! I hadn't thought this through at all.

Chapter Fifteen

Well, I wasn't going back home, that was definite. Mam would go mental—probably phone Grandad Martin straight away and tell him to bring his belt round. No way was I going back to that. Besides, I didn't have enough money for a return fare. I'd used up all my replica shirt money on the single ticket coming and only had the twenty quid Grandad had given me left over.

Instead, I walked back into Wakefield and spent the rest of the afternoon hanging round the city centre. Nobody gave me a second glance. It was the summer holidays, after all, so there were plenty of kids my age roaming round.

I ate some of my biscuits on a bench outside the cathedral, saving the crisps and cheese until later, then I walked round the streets exploring. I found Brody's posh girls' school up near a hospital and then had a quick nosy round an art gallery nearby. I felt dead proud because in three hours I hadn't spent any money and had still kept myself busy. Eventually I was bursting for the loo so I headed for the bus station. I used the facilities, washed my hands in the sink, then filled my water bottle from the tap. I wasn't daft enough to get caught without water, was I? And it was free— double result.

I checked my watch; it was just after six. Mam wouldn't even be home yet and here I was, already a hundred miles away. I thought about sending her a quick text to say I was fine but when I checked my mobile, it was as flat as a pancake because I hadn't recharged it since last week. Never mind, I thought; she couldn't care less anyway.

It was the rush hour now and people were milling

around catching buses home after work. It was then I saw the number thirty-nine which I knew was the one Alex always caught when she went into town. My heart skipped a beat. That was it! I could catch that bus and be outside Alex's house in ten minutes. She'd be back from After School club now and well pleased to see me! I could kip down on her bedroom floor for a few days and . . .

The smile faded. What if her mam answered the door? Or her dad? Or Caitlin? They'd give me a cup of tea then be on the phone to Mam quicker than you could say 'Headless Herbert'. I'd be back to square one. I couldn't risk it. Maybe I could call her from a phone box, though . . . arrange to meet her somewhere . . .

'Are you all right, lovey? You look a bit lost?'

I felt someone tug on my backpack and spun round to see an old geezer staring up at me from a bench. He had a whiskery chin and yellow, broken teeth. Tramp alert! 'I'm not your lovey,' I said, scowling at him to show I meant business.

He took a swig from a plastic cup and shrugged. 'Just askin' that's all. No harm in askin' is there? Why don't you sit here and talk to Old Duggan for two minutes? I could do with some company.' He patted the space next to him.

Not on your nelly, smelly, I thought. I was on the number thirty-nine bus in two seconds flat.

I wasn't sure where to get off so I waited until I recognized Alex's house then got off the stop after that. I knew I was on Zetland Avenue so I cut through a side street. It was still light. I didn't want to stray too far from Alex's but I didn't want to risk bumping into Mrs McCormack or anyone from the club, either. The side street I'd picked came to a dead end, with only a narrow alley down one side and a fenced-in field facing me. A fenced-in field? Yes! It was the school playing field—it had to be! I ran down the alley, knowing now it led to the main entrance to the school.

I was right. One–nil to Nevin. As I ran, the first thing that came into view was the top of the tepee in the Patch. The Patch! I slowed right down then, my heart pounding, as I walked parallel to the dense willow walls only a few metres across from the security fencing. Jolene, lass, I said to myself, you've found yourself a bed for the night.

I knew I'd never be able to climb over the security fence without being caught but luckily I didn't need to. I spied a gap under it where the mesh had buckled because someone or something—dogs probably—had dug beneath it. Luckily the end house adjoining the alley was boarded up and empty, so I knew I wouldn't be spotted by nosy neighbours from that side. Checking no one was around, I pushed my backpack up and through the gap and followed it, hoping digging was all the dogs had done in the hole.

I then pelted the short way towards the perimeter of the Patch, running round the willow fencing until I reached the gate and then, once inside, strode up to the door of the tepee, clicked open the door latch Sam Riley had so carefully designed, and let myself in.

I glanced round, trying to adjust to the gloom.

As far as I could make out, it was just an empty space apart from the beanbags scattered round the base of the tepee.

The ground and lower half of the wall had plastic sheeting to waterproof the place, overlaid with seagrass matting, so it wasn't damp or anything. Still, it wasn't what you'd call cosy either. I sighed. It would have to do for now.

Chapter Sixteen

I slept there that night and the night after that. It was easy, really. I knew Mrs McCormack and Mrs Fryston arrived about half past seven to set up the breakfast club for the early birds. All I did was make sure I was gone by then and creep back into the tepee after seven in the evening. I could carry on doing that for a few weeks until Grandad came home, no problem. I had already decided not to try to contact Alex. It would only put her in an awkward position and I knew what a rubbish fibber she was. Besides, I couldn't be much closer to her, could I? This was nearly as good as actually seeing her.

Funnily enough, it wasn't the night times that bothered me; I've never been scared of the dark or anything. It was the days. I hadn't bargained for how time would drag. Wakefield isn't as big as Sunderland or Newcastle and there isn't that much to do for twelve hours when you're on your own without much money.

On the third day, it rained all the time and I got soaked. I tried to get in to the afternoon showing at the cinema but when I reached the counter, I didn't have enough cash left to pay for a ticket. I'd tried to be careful with Grandad's twenty but a Big Mac here and bus fare there—that was it: I'd run out of money. I was skint already.

I trundled miserably round the Ridings Shopping Centre, slowly drying out but feeling hungrier and hungrier. I needed to sort myself out—fast.

When I woke up on the fourth morning, stiff

and tired, I ached all over and couldn't stop shivering. I closed my eyes, which burnt behind the lids. I forced myself to get up from the middle of the floor and dumped the beanbags I'd slept on back in their place. Today, I reckoned, I'd check out Grandad's house again. There might be a back way I could get in and even his potting sheds had to be better than this. Besides, I'd begun to change my mind about being so close to Alex. What was the point of being so near to her and the After School club when I couldn't see her or join in with anything? Talk about rubbing my nose in it.

I had just pushed the beanbag back into place when I heard a noise. I listened again. There was definitely someone coming up the path—not just one person, either, loads of them. Their footsteps crunched noisily on the gravel. I checked my watch and nearly died on the spot. It was eight o'clock already! What were they doing coming in here, though? It was still early.

I dived under the nearest beanbags for cover, frantically pulling them over me so I just had enough air to breathe. It's a good job I did because seconds later the latch on the tepee door opened and in they came.

'Put the grub in the middle,' I heard Reggie order.

'What about the drinks?' Lloyd asked.

'Same, and wipe your feet on the mat, all of you,' ordered Reggie. Who'd died and made him king? I wondered, poking a tiny hole between the folds of the beanbag so I could breathe better. Oh, I felt totally bunged up. I hoped they wouldn't be long.

There was a lot of shuffling and banging about, then Alex spoke, and I had to force myself to stay still so that I didn't leap out and grab her. 'Shall we sit in a circle? Circles are best for discussions, I think.' Her voice was flat and empty.

'Yeah, whatever,' Reggie agreed.

'I'm going to shove something against the door in case Mrs Fryston comes.' That was bossy Sammie Wesley.

'What did you tell her we were doing?' Reggie asked.

'Planning where to put the sculptures.'

'Nice one,' Reggie said.

There was more shuffling and I realized people were dragging beanbags to the middle to sit on. I grabbed hold of the one covering me and hoped nobody would try to pull it away. My heart was racing but the good thing about having anger-management lessons is you get taught how to breathe, slow and deep, to calm yourself down when you're feeling stressed. Well, I couldn't be any more stressed than this. I concentrated hard on my breathing; in through the nose, out through the mouth, in through the nose, out through the mouth. I didn't relax a muscle until I heard Reggie ask if everybody was ready and I knew my beanbag was safe. There was a chorus of yesses. 'OK, then,' he said, all solemn like the vicar who did our Tuesday assemblies at school, 'who wants to kick off?'

Chapter Seventeen

'I'll start,' I heard Lloyd say. 'I think we've got to work out what we'd do if we were running away. You know, put yourself in Jolene's place.'

My place? This whole meeting was about me? I was all ears now. 'If it were me,' Lloyd continued, 'I'd go down by the canal. There are loads of places to hide there. Even near where I live there's an empty lock-keeper's cottage. It's boarded up but you can get inside easily and it's dry. I've played in there loads of times with my brother Huw and his friends.'

Thanks for the tip, mush, I thought.

'No way!' Alex said in alarm. 'I'd hate it if she went there; it's too creepy and dangerous.'

'Anyway, the police have already searched round the canal,' Sammie Wesley added.

What? The police? What police? I forced my breathing to slow down as much as I could without it actually stopping.

'How do you know that?' Lloyd asked.

'It was on *Calendar News*, dingbat.'

'Well, I didn't know, did I? We don't all have televisions,' Lloyd replied, sounding offended.

'Did you see the interview with her mum? She was crying her eyes out,' Sammie continued in that tone people use when they are pretending to care but really they're just loving the drama.

'What do you expect?' Reggie snapped.

Sammie ignored him. 'I'm just giving Lloyd the details. He needs to know. Anyway, she was twisting Jolene's Sunderland shirt round and round in her hand, going "She'd never have gone without her shirt. If anything's happened to her, I don't know what I'll do; she's all I've got." My mum was in bits then. I had to pass her the tissues.

She said it's a mother's worst nightmare, having one of your kids go missing.'

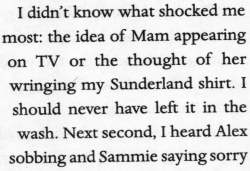

I didn't know what shocked me most: the idea of Mam appearing on TV or the thought of her wringing my Sunderland shirt. I should never have left it in the wash. Next second, I heard Alex sobbing and Sammie saying sorry and that she didn't mean to upset her. If they'd been giving out medals in willpower right then, I'd have got gold. How I managed to stay beneath that beanbag I'll never know. I felt sweat pouring down my face. I was cold and hot at the same time. There was too much to take in, especially when my head felt as if it was stuffed full of soggy Weetabix.

'Chin up, lass,' Reggie said, 'Jolene's tough, she'll be fine.'

'She's still only eleven,' Alex mumbled, and I could tell from her voice she was trying to hold herself together. 'I'm really worried. Nobody's seen her since Monday and today's Thursday.'

'If it *was* her that eyewitness saw in the bus station on Monday; we can't be sure,' Lloyd said.

What 'eyewitness'? That old geezer?

'I just don't get why she hasn't called Alex if she is in Wakefield like the police think. That's what I'd have done, first thing, called my best mate,' Sammie said.

'I know,' Alex mumbled, her voice cracking, 'I keep sitting by the phone, waiting and waiting. We all do.'

'She might not be able to get to a phone,' Lloyd pointed out.

'What about Brody? Have you got through to her yet?' Sam asked.

I swallowed hard. Brody? There was no need to bring her and Grandad into this. I was fine!

'Nah,' Reggie said, 'nothing. I reckon her mum meant it when she said no mobiles on holiday. It's just dead when I try to text her.'

'Like Jolene might be,' Sammie said dramatically.

Everyone shouted at her to shut up.

'I'm just saying,' Sammie protested, sounding hurt.

There was a long silence. 'Well,' Reggie said finally, 'we'd best get back to After School club before Mrs Fryston sends out search parties for us, too. Unless anyone's got anything to say? Anything *constructive.*'

Nobody had but I let out this mighty sneeze. It was a good one; made them all jump ten foot into the air. Very constructive.

Chapter Eighteen

Five minutes later I was sitting in the middle of the circle, sneezing and shivering. Alex had her arms wrapped round me and so did Sammie. Reggie was pacing up and down saying, 'Flaming Nora! Under our noses all the time! Wicked!'

'She's freezing,' Sammie said, 'give her your jumpers everyone.'

'I'll do it, I'll do it!' Alex told Sammie, pushing her away as Sammie tried to tuck the sweatshirts and cardigans round my knees.

'Oh, Jolene. You are in so much trouble!' Reggie laughed.

The others told
him to belt
up but I knew
he was right.
This wasn't like
last time I'd run away at all. That was nothing
compared to this. The police were out looking
for me—Mam had been on the telly—I was in
trouble all right. Up to my neck and rising.

'Jolene, what do you want to do now?' Alex asked.

'I don't know,' I admitted. I turned to Sammie.
'Sammie, was anyone else with Mam when she
was on telly? Anyone sitting with her?'

'Er . . . yeah . . . I can't remember who they
said it was, though. He never said nothing.'

'Did he have a daft hairstyle—you know—
peroxide white and cut short?' I asked hopefully.

'No. It was grey, his hair. My mum said he
looked a bit . . .'

'A bit what?'

'Nothing.'

'A bit what?'

'A bit shifty.'

No guesses for who that was. Grandad Martin. Huh! He even managed to look shifty on television. My heart sank then. If it had been Darryl instead of Grandad Martin . . . But no, I thought, it wouldn't be, would it? *He* had enough to worry about.

'Shall I go get Mrs Fryston?' Alex asked.

'No!' I shouted. It came out louder and harsher than I meant.

'But you're shivery. You need . . .'

'No!' I repeated. 'I don't want her. I don't want anyone!'

I hugged my knees to my chest, rocking myself back and forth. One by one, they shuffled closer, keeping me warm. I looked at each of them in turn. 'Look, you lot, I know I shouldn't have come here, and I don't want to get you all done or anything but if you dob me in, I'll only run away again and this time to somewhere huge like London. That's definite, that is. All I'm asking is for you to hide me until Grandad comes back from America at the end of the month.'

Alex bit her lip and looked worried but Lloyd nodded. 'Fair enough,' he said.

'Yeah, but come on, Lloydy. Mrs Fryston will freak if she finds out,' Reggie began.

'Well, we've just got to make sure she doesn't find out then, haven't we?' Lloyd replied, his voice low and calm. I stared at him over my pile of jumpers, glad he seemed to understand. He reminded me of Keith. The sort that doesn't say much but when he does, people sit up and take notice. 'This is what I think,' Lloyd continued, 'Jolene's our friend, right?' Everyone nodded. 'Well, we should respect our friends and help them when they need help, even if it means not doing what grown-ups want us to do.'

I liked the way Lloyd thought. I couldn't have put it better myself.

'I don't know,' Reggie said, staring at me.

'What's to know?' Lloyd asked. 'Listen, you lot. Aren't you fed up with being told what to do all the time? Everywhere you go it's do this, do that, eat this, don't eat that. One minute you're too old to be playing on the swings, the next minute you're too young to be out alone in the playground. You can't even go fishing in peace without someone asking you why you're there and how old you are. There's no freedom any more. When my grandad was little he used to walk six miles to school on his own in the dark. Now kids aren't allowed to sneeze without somebody making a rule against it. Grown-ups tell us what to do all the time. What happened to letting us make our own decisions? Make our own mistakes, too, maybe, but at least they're our own mistakes.'

Like a football manager's pep-talk at half-time, Lloyd's inspirational speech did the trick. Everyone nodded and muttered things like 'He's right' and Sammie moaned her mum even asked her what she was doing when she was on the loo.

'So now what?' Reggie asked.

'Now we promise to stick together and help Jolene,' Lloyd replied. 'All in favour say "aye".'

Every one of them said 'aye', although Alex's 'aye' was a bit of a low one, but I reckoned she was still in shock at seeing me here. I couldn't blame her; I'd have been fazed too, I reckon.

'Thanks,' I whispered, giving them all a weak smile.

The mood lifted then. People began coming out with ideas about what to do and what to bring me. 'We need a password,' Reggie suggested, 'so Jolene knows it's one of us when we approach.'

Before anyone could come up with anything I sneezed again. 'There you go,' Reggie laughed, 'we'll sneeze—one for "it's us" and two for "danger".'

'And some sort of system for keeping watch. We should work in pairs, doing a stint each, so no one gets suspicious,' Lloyd said.

'What if somebody wants to use the tepee?' Sam asked.

'It's only meant to be used by the older ones anyway and seeing as we are the older ones . . .' Reggie said.

'Since when has that stopped your Ruby?' Sammie snorted.

'The girl has a point,' Reggie admitted.

'We'll have to block the entrance somehow. Or fiddle with the latch so no one can get in,' Lloyd said, immediately going towards the door and examining the keyhole. He was all fired up, this one.

'Someone should make a list of supplies and that—food and stuff,' Sammie then suggested.

'Hell, yes,' Reggie nodded, rubbing his hands together, 'we'll do all those! At last, something exciting happens at After School club. Bring it on!'

Chapter Nineteen

They left soon after, promising to be back as soon as they could. 'We'll be close by anyway, setting up the sculpture park,' Alex told me. I just nodded and pulled the beanbags up to my chin, glad I didn't have to trail round Wakefield again and could lie down in peace.

Half an hour later, the commotion started as the whole of After School club descended on the Patch. I had made myself a little nest with the beanbags close to the window and was happy just listening, working out who was where from my hiding place. There was plenty of banging and scraping and hammering. Mrs Fryston was going round each group, saying the usual things. 'That's fantastic!' 'Oh, Ruby, what a good idea!' 'Lloyd, what can I say? I love how you've angled the wheel so it catches the light. You are so talented.'

A tall shadow against the door startled me for a second until I realized it was Headless Herbert. I grinned, eager to hear what Mrs Fryston had to say about him.

'Oh, doesn't he look imposing!' she said but then added, 'Don't you think he needs to be a bit more to the side? He's blocking the door to the tepee a bit too much.'

'Oh, he looks cool just there, Mrs Fryston.'

I realized what Alex was doing then; she was using Headless Herbert as a guard to stop anyone barging in and finding me.

'Cool, yes, but I think you need to shuffle him across, just a tiny bit.'

Lloyd joined in then. 'Actually, it's perfect there, Mrs Fryston. He unifies the dynamics of the whole sculpture park. He acts as a beacon, harmonizing colour, shape, and space. To move him even a millimetre would be to destroy that fragile synchronicity.'

'Well,' Mrs Fryston said, and I could tell she didn't have a clue what he was talking about either, 'if you say so.'

She then disappeared to find another group to praise.

A few seconds later, I heard a sneeze and something dropped through the window, landing on my lap. A packet of aspirins! These guys thought of everything. I snug- gled down in my  beanbags. Everything would be fine now. Every- thing would be mint.

I didn't leave the tepee the rest of the day. I had plenty to eat and drink from the stores the gang had brought in first thing and the aspirins had brought my temperature right down.

Next morning, I was feeling fit again, and was well perked up by the time I heard the sneezes outside and the gang trooped in. 'Mornin', Hermit,' Reggie greeted me, 'we've brought prezzies.'

'Top,' I smiled, looking round for Alex but not finding her.

'Alex isn't in yet—she's helping her mum do something,' Sammie said, as if reading my mind.

'OK,' I said, shuffling upright to check out my presents.

Reggie plonked himself down next to me. 'Right, then. Sam first.'

Sam produced a carrier bag. 'Er . . . I've brought you some stationery and pens from our shop in case you want to write letters or draw or something . . . and some breakfast bars nobody else likes at home.'

'Thanks.'

Reggie handed over a small cardboard box. 'I've brought you my Walkman to listen to. You can only borrow it, though. I want it back after. I've put loads of decent tapes in and spare batteries. How thoughtful am I?'

'Very. Thanks, Reggie.'

Sammie kneeled down in front of me, pulling

a bag from the inside of her jacket. 'Well,' she said, unrolling it, 'I noticed your hair was a right mess yesterday so I've brought you my second best hairbrush to borrow . . .' She was about to hand it over when she paused. 'You haven't got nits have you?'

'No.'

'OK then. And here's some wipes for your face and some clean knickers.' She leaned closer and whispered, though her whisper was still loud enough for everyone to hear. 'I don't mean to be embarrassin' or nothing but it's a girl thing, isn't it? Don't worry, they're brand new. I got them for my birthday but they're too small so I thought they might fit you, seeing as you're so skinny. They've got hearts on, see.'

'Er . . . great . . . yeah.'

'I've got some just the same as them,' Reggie joked, 'they fit like a glove.'

'You shouldn't even be looking!' Sammie said, stuffing the cellophane bag hurriedly away.

As each person brought my booty, the others stood watch round the door. Last up was Lloyd.

He shrugged a heavy rucksack from his back and began producing one thing after another. Torch, a compass, a blanket, a rolled-up sleeping bag, a book called *The Worst Case Scenario*—just in case, he said—small cartons of fruit juice, dried fruit, biscuits. It went on and on. 'Blimey,' I said when he'd finished, 'have you anything left at your house?'

Lloyd shrugged. 'It's only what I take when I camp out.'

'You're ace, you know that, don't you?' I told them all. 'True mates.'

Chapter Twenty

I didn't see Alex until much later. Half five, six o'clock-ish. 'Nice of you to turn up,' I joked as she sneaked in.

'I . . . I can't stay long,' she said, glancing behind her every two seconds, 'Mum and Mrs Fryston are clearing away . . . I said I'd just check the sculptures were OK.'

'Well, sit down, take a load off,' I said, pulling a spare beanbag up for her.

Alex shook her head. 'I can't. They might come looking.'

I sighed. I was feeling bored and wanted Alex

just to sit and relax with me for a second. Why did she have to be so uptight? 'OK, suit yourself,' I told her grumpily.

She began pacing up and down in front of me. 'Are you sure you want to do this, Jolene?'

'Do what?'

'Stay here hiding.'

'Course. I've got everything I need, why shouldn't I?'

'But . . . don't you want me to make a phone call to . . . to people, to let them know you're OK?'

'No, I don't.'

'Why not?'

'Because then it'll take them about two minutes to find me! I know what you're like, Alex. You're rubbish when people start asking loads of questions.'

The pacing stopped instantly. 'I'm not. I'm quite good, actually,' she said, all defensive.

'Yeah, whatever.'

She became even more grumpy and began the pacing up and down thing again which was beginning to get on my nerves. 'How will you manage until Monday?' she then asked.

'What do you mean?'

'It's Friday today . . . nearly the weekend.'

I frowned. I hadn't thought of that. Two days was a long time without visitors. 'You'll come, won't you? Sneak out for half an hour tomorrow or Sunday?'

She shook her head. 'I . . . no, I can't. We've got . . . we've got guests staying.'

Charming! Here I was, living in a blinking hut only two minutes walk from her house and she couldn't even be bothered to check how I was. After all I'd been through. 'Thanks a bunch, Alex,' I snapped. The pacing increased and I reached out my hand and grabbed her ankle to stop her. 'Pack it in, you're doing my head in!' I told her.

'Sorry,' she said, almost losing her balance but finally stopping and sitting opposite me.

Neither of us spoke for a minute. 'Please come and see me, Alex. I'll be lonely otherwise,' I said.

She shook her head. 'I can't. They'd notice if I left.'

'They'd notice if I left,' I mimicked, angry at her. Flipping heck, if it was the other way round, I'd be here every second I could, I would. Some mate she was turning out to be in an emergency.

Alex leapt to her feet then. 'I'd better go,' she said, marching towards the door.

'Yeah, you had,' I told her. 'Have a nice weekend, won't you?'

Chapter Twenty-One

As if to match my mood, it rained all weekend. I just sat huddled in Lloyd's sleeping bag, listening to it pelting down, watching the water drip. On Monday morning, the first thing Sam asked me when they all trooped in was if the tepee had leaked. 'It's been its first proper test,' he said.

'Loads, especially that part there,' I told him, pointing out the boggy patch beneath the window.

'Are you sure it's from the rain and not you?' Reggie grinned.

'Cheek! I go . . . you know . . . outside when it's dark. Over by the bush thing.'

'Oh, flipping heck! Spare me the details.'

'You asked,' I told him.

They all started talking about how I should use the loo then! 'We could bring you a bucket,' Lloyd said, 'or maybe a spade—so you can just dig a hole and cover it up again. That's probably more eco-friendly. No loo roll, though. That'd be a give-away and anyway, it's unnecessary. The Romans used to use a . . .'

Sam interrupted the history lesson. 'Hang on a minute; next year's Year Sixes have got to work in here in September. They don't want to be sitting on piles of you-know-what.'

'Do y'mind? I don't do piles! I'm not a carthorse!' I said, turning to face Alex, who had so far not said a thing. 'What about you, Alex? Any good ideas?'

'No,' she mumbled, scraping her foot across the seagrass matting. She'd better not start the pacing thing or I'd thump her.

'I didn't think you would have,' I said, still annoyed at her for not bothering to visit me at all over the weekend. It had been a long, long two days.

She stared glumly at the floor. What was with her? She'd turned into such a mardy. 'Oh, cheer up, Alex,' I told her. 'It's not like *you've* got to wee in a hole, is it?'

She glowered at me, good and proper. I was a bit taken aback, I admit it. Alex never gave me dirty looks. 'You think this is just a joke, don't you, Jolene?' she asked.

'Yeah, if you say so.'

She flung her arms round the room, pointing out all the stuff I'd got scattered about. 'And the rest of you are just as bad, running round after her like she was some lost little princess when you know people are out there, looking for her, worried sick!'

'Well, if that's how you feel, don't come any more,' Sammie told her.

'Yeah, Alex. Go get a life!' I snarled.

'Fine by me!' she said and left, just like that.

'What's eating her?' Sammie asked, handing me a toffee.

'Who cares,' I shrugged, 'I've got more important things to worry about.'

'Follow her, Lloydy,' Reggie said, 'get her to calm down or she'll blow it.'

'OK.'

Reggie looked at Sammie and me then, shaking his head. 'Way to go, you two. So much for sticking together.'

'Sorry, Reg,' Sammie said instantly.

I just stared at the floor. He needn't think he was making me feel bad about Alex. She knew more than anyone what it was like for me with Mam and Grandad Martin back home. Pity she couldn't remember because, until she did, *we* weren't talking.

Reggie moved over to the door. 'Come on, we'd better do what we were meant to do; check out the sculptures for rain damage. Someone'll be over at lunch with your sandwiches later, Jolene.'

'Right,' I said.

He stepped outside, followed by Sam and Sammie. I followed them, peering out as far as I dared. It was much sunnier today but there were still plenty of puddles where the uneven pathway dipped. I took a gulp of fresh air before Sam closed the door, an apologetic look on his face.

'Well, Headless Herbert's had it for starters,' I heard Reggie say.

'Why?' I asked, as loudly as I dared, my face pressed close to the latticed door frame.

'Half the mod rock's come unstuck and his neck's filled with water. He looks like a mummy gone wrong.'

'Oh.'

'Or a very weird bird bath.'

'Ha!' I laughed. So much for Alex's finishing him off properly.

The three of them spent a couple more minutes inspecting the sculptures. I tried tracking them, moving round inside the tepee while they moved round outside. It gave me something to do. The blind on the window rustled and a toffee dropped onto the floor. 'That's gone in the mud now!' I

 told Sammie striding across to that side.

'Soz—I forgot,' she whispered.

'No worries. Hey, if you can get me some mints next time.'

'Oh-oh.'

'What?'

'Lloyd's here and he looks . . .'

'What?'

'Hide, Jolene, hide quick!'

Chapter Twenty-Two

I scrambled beneath the beanbags and waited, my heart thumping in my chest. There was a lot of scraping around and heated whispering but I couldn't make anything out. Then the door opened and closed again quickly and Lloyd began firing instructions at me. 'Wherever you are stay hidden and don't move. As soon as you get the signal, run for it.'

I wanted to ask what signal but he was still in full flow. 'Mrs Fryston heard me talking to Alex about you outside the mobile. She asked what was going on and I said nothing but Alex burst out crying. I've got the feeling she'll crack.'

Yeah, I thought, clenching my fist, me too.

Lloyd didn't speak again but seemed to be shifting things round all over the place. It was the same outside; what were they doing? Reorganizing the whole of the sculpture park? The answer to that must have been yes because a few seconds later I heard Mrs Fryston's voice, asking Reggie to move this and that back to where it came from. She didn't sound angry or anything. At first.

'Don't you think the stuff looks better like this, Mrs F? All clustered together? We do, don't we, guys?'

'Yeah, we do,' Sammie and Sam chorused.

'Move it all away from the door, please.'

'Can't, Mrs F. Especially Herbert. He's undergoing emergency repairs.'

'Well, do the repair job over there, Reggie. I want to look inside the tepee.'

'Can't shift him. The water's weighed him down . . .'

There was a loud scraping and I heard Sammie gasp and Reggie go, 'Blooming heck, Mrs Fryston, have you been going to the gym?'

I had to begin my breathing exercises then, because I knew she was on her way in and I knew she knew what she was going to find. The latch clicked and I sensed her stepping inside. 'Ah, Lloyd,' Mrs Fryston said, her tone not quite as patient by now.

'Hi,' Lloyd replied.

'Would you mind standing up, please. I'd like to check beneath that heap of things you've got stacked up there.'

'Why?'

'Just move please, Lloyd.'

'Nah! I'm happy here, thanks.'

'Well, I'm far from happy that you're here. You should be over in the mobile, like I asked.'

'Happy here.'

Mrs Fryston took a deep breath then, as if to gather all her patience together. 'Lloyd, I need you to move,' she said in a firm voice.

I was so busy listening to Lloyd and Mrs Fryston that I didn't feel the tug on my beanbag at first. Then it came again. And again. Followed by a kick. Mrs Fryston wasn't the only one wanting someone to move. I got it then: the signal. Lloyd's pile was the decoy, giving me a chance to escape. Slowly, like a tortoise reversing, I began to back out, edging bit by bit along the walls of the tepee. I made it as far as the door and even managed to get to the outside. It was when I tried to stand up and run for it I came unstuck. I was squinting so much in the daylight that I tripped straight over Herbert's metal base which sent me flying onto the gravel. By the time I was on my feet, Mrs Fryston had her arms round my shoulders and as much as I tried to twist and turn, I could not escape from her grasp. 'Get off me,' I kept yelling, 'you aren't allowed to touch me!'

'No you're not,' Lloyd said, standing in front of us and looking angrily at her.

Mrs Fryston just gripped me closer and began bellowing at him at the top of her lungs. 'Be quiet, Lloyd! And that goes for all of you! You are all in enough trouble as it is! Now get over to that mobile. This instant!'

I was used to teachers shouting at me but even I jumped then. It was more scary, somehow, coming from Mrs Fryston, who never lost her temper. The effect on the others was immediate. Sammie and Sam both went bright red and looked nervously at each other and even Reggie couldn't think of a comeback this time. Instead he walked over to Lloyd and nudged him. 'Come on, mate. Let's go.'

Lloyd's eyes watered and he glanced at me. 'Sorry, Jolene,' he said.

'Don't worry about it,' I told him, 'it's Alex that'll be sorry.'

Chapter Twenty-Three

The funniest bit that happened next was when Mrs Fryston marched us into the mobile and everybody in there carried on as normal. Brandon even came up to me and said, 'Oh, hello, Jolene, want to play sharks?'

Mrs Fryston told him 'Not right now, Brandon,' and made him go to one of the playleaders. She then clapped her hands and announced that she wanted everyone to go outside and get some fresh air before lunch. The playleaders, noticing me for the first time, quickly started shepherding the kids into the playground. Alex, I realized, was not among them and nor was Mrs McCormack. Coward, I thought. Running home with Mummy.

As soon as the last kid had left I expected Mrs Fryston to start blasting us all again but instead she reached out and began checking my hands. 'That was a nasty fall,' she said, looking at the grit and scraped skin on my palms. She told Sammie to fetch the first aid box. 'Are you OK, Jolene?' Mrs Fryston asked.

I shrugged. 'It's only a few scratches. I get worse playing football in the park.'

'No, I mean, are you OK? You're not hurt? Or injured? From anything that's happened to you in the past week?'

I shook my head and she let out a sigh of relief. 'Thank goodness for that.' Sammie brought the first aid box and Mrs Fryston began to clean my hands, all the time asking us questions in her old, calm manner.

Nobody tried to fib. There was no point. In the end, Mrs Fryston shook her head. 'Well, I wondered why the tepee had gone from "flavour of the month" one minute to "a boring dump" the next and now I know. I can't believe I never cottoned on. Oh, what a mess.'

'Are we in big trouble, Mrs Fryston?' Sammie asked. Her bottom lip was going; the waterworks would start any second. I knew from last summer this girl could fill dams.

Mrs Fryston gave her a little smile but didn't deny it. 'Well, I will have to call the police soon and they will want to talk to all of you. And I have to warn you they won't treat what you did as a game, Sammie.'

'Good, because it wasn't a game! We were helping a friend,' Lloyd said, his whole body tense. The lad was still pumped up and I felt glad I had one fighter still left on the team. That would come in useful. Now that I'd got over being discovered, I was planning my next move.

Mrs Fryston gave Sammie the first aid box to put back and told her to go wash her face, sending Sam with her for company, before she replied to Lloyd. Her voice was warm and sympathetic. 'I'm sorry, Lloyd. I didn't mean to patronize you. I know it wasn't a game to you, and I admire your loyalty, but you have to see all sides. The police have spent hours searching the city for Jolene.'

'So? That's their job! At least she's alive, so that's a result, right?'

Mrs Fryston's face was a picture then! She looked so shocked because Lloyd wasn't being a good little boy and backing down but I don't know why she should have been. I mean, the kid was home-schooled. His parents encouraged him to be independent. He camped out; he used a knife to gut fish he'd caught by himself. He wasn't a follower like the others. Like Alex. Oh, my blood boiled when I thought of her. What a wimp she'd turned out to be. What a snitch. The sparks started in my head the more I thought about her. But the sparks were bad news; they made me lash out and do stupid things. I had to stay focused. Five currant buns. Five currant buns in a baker's shop . . .

'Jolene? Jolene?' Mrs Fryston repeated, touching my arm.

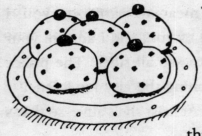

'Sorry, miles away, miss,' I said and gave her a little, feeble smile. I had to keep it polite. Make her think I was just going to sit here and wait for the police to lecture me and send me back to Mam.

'I asked why, Jolene. Why did you run away?'

I just shrugged and stared at the floor. 'I don't know, miss. I was just being silly, I suppose.'

I don't think she knew what to say to that. Instead she told us all to sit down for a minute and she reached into her handbag and took out her mobile. Reggie perked up then. 'I'm innocent! I demand to see my lawyer!' he joked, thinking, like we all did, she was calling the police. Mrs Fryston held her hand up for him to be quiet and started talking into her phone. Reggie plonked himself down, looking deflated.

'Andrew?' Mrs Fryston said. 'Are you still in your office? Brilliant! Can you come across to the mobile, please . . . something's cropped up.'

That's handy, isn't it? Being married to the headteacher of the school, especially one who spends his summer holidays sorting out paperwork. Andrew—Mr Sharkey—was over before you could say 'busted'. It was going to be harder to do a runner now, that was for sure.

While the missus brought him up to speed with the good news, I glanced round. I was about ten strides away from the door, that was all, but I could see Sammie standing on the other side of it, dabbing her eyes and talking to Sam. The pair of them were blocking my exit. Well, tough. They'd just have to shift or get trampled on, wouldn't they? I rose slowly from my seat. If anybody asked, I was going to the bogs.

I managed one step before I felt a hand on my shoulder. 'Jolene, I want you to come somewhere with me,' Mrs Fryston said.

Bogger, I thought. Bogger, bogger, bogger.

'Jan, I think you're making a mistake. You should wait until the police get here,' Mr Sharkey told her, frowning at me.

She waved a set of car keys at him. 'I know, I

know, but I think it's important to do this first. Give me five minutes.'

'Jan!'

'Five minutes.'

Chapter Twenty-Four

It took only two of the five minutes to get to Alex's house.

'What are we doing here?' I asked, scowling as Mrs Fryston levered me out of the back of her car.

'There's something here I think you should see. Or someone,' she said, pressing the doorbell.

I began struggling then, trying to free myself. 'If you think I'm apologizing to that tell-tale, you've got another think coming. In fact, I wouldn't even let me go in there, if I were you.'

'Well, it's a risk I'm willing to take,' Mrs Fryston

said gripping me firmly. Reggie was right, I reckoned; she had been going to the gym.

Mrs McCormack opened the door and her hand flew to her mouth when she saw me. 'Oh, Jolene,' she said and she had the same catch in her voice as Mrs Fryston had when she'd cleaned my scratches. Like she really cared I was OK. Not that I cared that she cared. Not one bit.

'Y'all reet, Mrs McCormack?' I mumbled.

'Are they still here?' Mrs Fryston asked her, pulling me with her into the house.

'Yes,' Mrs McCormack replied, 'we were just getting ready to come to you.'

I was concentrating too hard on not losing focus to work out what they were talking about. This wasn't the nice house where I'd had good times in the past, I kept telling myself. Being here was like being among Toon supporters at St James's Park as far as I was concerned—deep into enemy territory. Mrs Fryston stopped at the hat stand and turned to smile at me. 'Go with Ann, Jolene, but you haven't got long. I do have to take you back in a minute.'

'Whatever,' I muttered, following Mrs McCormack towards the living room.

I had hardly stepped through the doorway when I heard screams, followed by the thunder of feet, and before I had time to catch my breath, I was being whirled in the air by a big bloke with a bristly chin. While he was doing that, two lads were pulling at my legs, yelling and shouting.

'Jolene! Jolene! Thank God!' Darryl cried.

'Put her down! We want to hold her!' Jack protested.

Darryl did as he was told, plonking me down on the carpet, and next thing I knew I was being smothered by Jack and Keith. My brain kept throwing out little words like 'what?' and 'but!' and 'how?' but I never managed to say any of them.

The next part was all a bit of a blur, to be honest. Darryl was talking so fast and I was still dazed from the speed of everything since being found, it was hard to take everything in at once.

I'll tell you what I remember Darryl telling me. Darryl and the lads had been staying at Alex's since last Friday—they were who those guests had been. It turned out he had found out Alex's family's number from Directory Enquiries and been calling them since the police suspected I was in the area, just in case the McCormacks heard anything. Apparently my mam wouldn't talk to Darryl; she'd been telling everyone it was his fault I had run off in the first place so he had no right to know anything from her. Anyway, Darryl mentioned to Mrs McCormack how the lads were convinced I was hiding in the Yorkshire Sculpture Park we'd visited and how desperate they were to have a look for themselves. 'The police don't know the good hiding places,' Jack had kept saying. In the end, because she thought it might help, Mrs McCormack had suggested they come up for the weekend. 'We spent all day Saturday and all day Sunday searching, didn't we, lads?'

Jack and Keith nodded, their heads bobbing like seals in water.

'We got absolutely drenched on both days. We

should have gone back yesterday but Jacko here came down with a temperature, didn't you? We had a right night with him, daft lad.'

'I'm better now!' Jack cried as he clung to me, but when I looked at him properly, I could see that his face was pasty and he looked washed out. But then so did Keith and so did Darryl. It hit me, then, why Alex had been in a mardy with me. I glanced round, seeing her for the first time standing by the mantelpiece, watching us all. Her eyes were red from crying.

'Did you go to the Sculpture Park too?' I asked her.

She just nodded and wiped her eyes with the back of her sleeve. 'Both days,' she said.

'I'm sorry, Alex,' I told her, my voice cracking, 'I never thought anyone would come looking for me. I thought nobody cared.'

'Well, you got that wrong!' she said.

'Well wrong!' Keith added.

'I know,' I said, patting him but looking directly at Alex and feeling totally ashamed of myself for the things I'd called my best mate. 'I was out of order—you know—in the tepee. I wish I could undo everything—cast a spell or something to go back in time.'

'Like Tinkerbell can,' Jack whispered.

Alex just nodded. 'I know,' she said.

'We all wish that, hinny,' Darryl said. 'I don't know how many times I've wished I could turn the clock back and not say what I said to you at work that day.'

'Honest?' I asked.

His face tightened. 'It makes me shudder every time I think about it. You caught me at a really bad time, Jolene. I'd just been told by the solicitors if I didn't find a place soon, Tracie could get the lads living with her full time and he'd told me as far as you were concerned I had no chance because you weren't my biological daughter. Oh, I was in such a state. "But I love her like she's my own," I said, "and the lads love her like a sister." Then when you came flying in, so full of beans . . . oh, I didn't know what to say for the best and I got it totally wrong, like the idiot I am.'

I just stared when he said that. All right, I cried.

Cried more than Sammie Waterworks Wesley, if you must know. We all did.

'Hey,' Darryl said, wiping the tears on my face with his thumb and making me laugh, 'the good news is we've got a council flat in Lamesley. We move in at the end of August. How about that, then?'

'That's mint.'

'You can see the Angel of the North outside your bedroom window!' Keith said.

'My bedroom window?'

'For when you come and stay,' Darryl smiled.

Mrs Fryston knocked on the door and interrupted then, which is a good job otherwise Mrs McCormack's living room would have been flooded. 'I'm sorry, everybody, but it's time to call Jolene's mum now and the police. We have to go.'

I didn't argue. Whatever happened next didn't matter now. I knew Darryl and the lads loved me and Alex was my friend again and that was all that counted.

Epilogue

If you're expecting me to go into loads of details about what happened next, I can't. I can tell you some of it, just to wind everything up properly, like, but if you want the real nitty-gritty you'll have to ask someone else. Sorry and all that but I'm stressed out because school starts tomorrow and I haven't got half my stuff ready *and* I've got to see counsellor-lady again after my little adventure. So much for a fresh start at secondary school but, like Mam said, what did I expect when my face had been plastered all over the local papers? Counsellor-lady needn't be thinking she's getting more cakes out of me, that's all I can say.

I suppose giving you a run-down isn't such a bad idea. It'll be good preparation in case I have to write about what I did in the holidays. As if I'm telling!

I'll kick off with the police thing. Now *that* was a right hoo-ha. They asked me thousands of questions, searched the tepee, told me that no matter how bad things seemed at home, running away was never the answer, and that if I ever had problems again I should phone the *Childline* number. I told them not to worry, because running away is ninety-nine per cent boring anyway and I had no plans to repeat the exercise. They said that was good to hear because next time I might not be so lucky and, though I hate to admit it, I know they're right.

Reggie, Sammie, Sam, and Lloyd got a lecture too, about how they might have *thought* they were doing the right thing but in fact they weren't actually helping matters at all. I wasn't there when they got their talking to, otherwise I'd have complained because I didn't see why they should get done because of me. Apparently everyone was petrified apart from Lloyd who kept making a point about how we were all free to make our own choices, even if we were only ten or eleven years old, whether it inconvenienced authority or not. If you ask me, Lloyd Fountain's going to be famous one day. Or prime minister—one or the other.

Then, of course, there was Mam. She arrived with Grandad Martin later that evening and everything happened just exactly like I told you it would. She was all over me like a rash at first, kissing me and sobbing buckets and showing me my Sunderland shirt that she'd kept under her pillow every night. It was in a terrible state—all smudged from where her mascara had rubbed off. Honestly. She told the police—not for the first time, by the sound of it—that I'd run away because her ex-husband had been heartless and dumped me just like he'd dumped her. When I said, well, it wasn't just that, was it, what about you going on the cruise ships and making me change schools, she gave one of her fake laughs and said, 'Oh, Jolene. I was never serious about that, you silly thing.'

As soon as we got in the car she had a go at me for showing her up. 'Here's me just happy to see my baby alive and what happens? She makes up lies about me.' Course Grumpy Grandad Martin stuck his oar in then and said what did she expect? I'd always been a bad 'un, right from the start. I told him to put a sock in it and he told me if I didn't watch out I'd end up in care. I told him I'd rather be put in care with Dracula than live with him and Nana so he stopped the car on the hard shoulder of the motorway and would have given me a right back hander if Mam hadn't stopped him. That was a first, her sticking up for me.

To be fair, she's been a lot better with me since I came back. I think it really did frighten her when I ran away this time and she was upset when I'd made it so obvious I preferred Darryl to her. 'Broke my heart, that did,' she kept telling me. I suppose I had been a bit harsh on her but, like when I first heard about her and Darryl splitting up and I wasn't very sympathetic, when you've been let down by someone as often as I have, that's just how it is. You kind of stop feeling anything for the person. And it's not as if she's turned into a sweet as apple pie mam since, either. Don't worry, she still loses it and cracks me one when I wind her up but it's not as often. She's way less stressed now there's just the two of us and Grandad Jake gave her some money for bills.

What else. Oh, Darryl and the lads, of course. Well, in the beginning Mam still had the hump with Darryl so when he phoned the first few times to check out how I was and if he could take me to the footy, she just hung up on him. Then Mandy and Risa came back on the scene because their cruise had been cancelled due to food poisoning and she wanted to go on all-nighters with them. Mam daren't leave me alone in case I ran off again and Grandad Martin refused to have me (ooh, I was so gutted, I was) so she let Darryl stay over and look after me a couple of weekends and then when he moved into his new flat, I stayed over there. I stay most weekends now. The new place needs a bit of work but Darryl will soon have it sorted. Keith's already filled his side of the bedroom with car posters and Jack's filled his side with Peter Pan ones. We're just waiting for my Sunderland AFC wallpaper to arrive then we can get started on mine. You know, I hope Lloyd does become prime minister because then he can change the law so that top blokes like Darryl get the same rights as real dads if they split up from your mam. It's not fair otherwise, is it?

What else, what else? Nothing really. I don't hear much from Alex now, though she did invite me to the end of the holidays party they had at After School club. I told her I couldn't go because it was too far to come but really I didn't fancy it. If I'm honest, it hasn't been the same with Alex since that last time I saw her at her house, even though I said sorry and everything. I've talked to Brody about it and she says it's like when you break a favourite pot and glue it back again. It kind of looks the same but it's never quite right. Brody told me I missed a fun party though. Because so many people were leaving—her, Reggie, Sammie, and Sam—Mrs Fryston really pushed the boat out and hired a disco and everything. I hadn't realized all four of them were leaving—I'd have sent them something if I had—but it figures. Sam and Sammie are like me, in Year Seven next, and Brody and Reggie are Year Eight. I can't see me going back to that After School club again, either. You have to move on, don't you?

The times I do feel close to Alex are when I'm staying over at Darryl's and I look out of my bedroom window. Keith was spot-on, you can see the Angel of the North—just—if you stand on a chair and use binoculars. It's not the Angel I see, though, it's Headless Herbert, and when I think of him I think of that afternoon I spent with Alex, laughing so much it hurt.

Oh well, haway then, and get your lip gloss on.

Jolene Nevin-Birtley

The girls are back...

Sammie's Back

—the girl who makes a wish (but then really wishes she hadn't)

Helena Pielichaty

It wasn't my fault!

All I did was try to bring everyone together again.
I just wanted it to be how it used to be—before dad left.
That's not so wrong, it is?

But as usual, it all went pear-shaped. Why does
everything I do turn into a complete nightmare?
I feel like such an idiot.

I bet everyone else's families are perfect. Well, they
would be, wouldn't they—their lives are all brilliant
compared to mine . . .

ISBN-13: 978-0-19-275377-9
ISBN-10: 0-19-275377-0

Life sucks!

Everyone's always depending on me—Brody the Reliable. Expecting me to sort out their problems, but when I need help even my best buddy lets me down. Well, fine, if that's how he wants to play it, he can take a hike.

And that goes for all the others too. I'm through doing things just to please other people, and that includes being captain for the Big Book Quiz. Let Mrs Fryston find some other loser . . .

ISBN-13: 978-0-19-275378-6
ISBN-10: 0-19-275378-9

Alex's Back

—the girl who's trying
to keep life simple
(but simply can't do it)

Helena Pielichaty

What a nightmare!

*All I want is a quiet life—but do you think that's possible?
No chance.*

*It started off fine. With one best friend and out-of-school stuff
kept to almost zero, I had no worries. But then it all went
wrong. First there was the secret, then the secret about the
secret . . . and now everything's out of control!*

*The only time I feel calm is when I'm talking to my brother
Daniel—at least he never answers back. OK, so he's been
dead for years, but I don't have a problem with that—
unfortunately my family obviously does . . .*

ISBN-13: 978-0-19-275279-6
ISBN-10: 0-19-275279-7

Helena Pielichaty (pronounced Pierre-li-hatty) was born in Stockholm, Sweden, but most of her childhood was spent in Yorkshire. Her English teacher wrote of her in Year Nine that she produced 'lively and quite sound work but she must be careful not to let the liveliness go too far.' Following this advice, Helena never took her liveliness further south than East Grinstead, where she began her career as a teacher. She didn't begin writing until she was 32. Since then, Helena has written many books for Oxford University Press. She lives in Nottinghamshire with her husband and two children.

www.helena-pielichaty.com